www.enchantedlion.com

First English-language edition,
published in 2022
by Enchanted Lion Books,
248 Creamer Street,
Studio 4, Brooklyn, NY 11231

First published in France
as *Adieu Blanche-Neige*
Original French edition
copyright © 2021 by La Partie
English-language translation
copyright © 2022
by Enchanted Lion Books
Cover design by Eugenia Mello
All rights reserved under
International and Pan-American
Copyright Conventions
A CIP is on record with the
Library of Congress
ISBN 978-1-59270-381-4
Printed in China
by Toppan Leefung

First Printing

About Unruly

This is the second title to be published under Unruly, Enchanted Lion's new imprint of picture books that are innovative in form and narrative structure for older readers and adults.

We launched Unruly because we believe that we never age out of pictures and that the possibilities for the illustrated book are larger and richer than the categories that currently exist for it. Unruly celebrates the picture book as a unique medium of word and picture, of value to readers of all ages.

Through a text that sides with the shadows, and paintings that are as enthralling as they are unsettling, this picture book exposes the true ferocity of childhood stories, destabilizing notions of beauty and ugliness, good and evil.

We hope you enjoy it.

For the one who taught me
never to be afraid of painting.
—*Beatrice Alemagna*

Thank you to Béatrice Vincent, Pata le Grand, Emmanuel, Sandro, Yan, Eva, and Paul. Thank you to Jacob and Wilhelm Grimm. And thank you to the wonderstruck smile of Patricia, which will never fade.

Beatrice Alemagna

You can't Kill Snow White

Translated from French by
Karin Snelson and Emilie Robert Wong

an
Enchanted Lion Book
NEW YORK

The original text of Snow White was published for the first time in 1812, by the Brothers Grimm, in Germany.

There, you'll find no funny or lovestruck dwarves, no princely kisses, and no sugarcoated ending. The tale ends instead with the violent and merciless death of the queen, burned alive at Snow White's wedding as the guests look on.

What, I wondered, was at the heart of the original Grimm tale? Was it only about a villain? Was goodness nowhere to be found? This is why I wanted to shift the story's point of view to the queen—to close in on her suffering, jealousy, and vengeance.

To side with darkness as a way of understanding the madness.

PRE

To speak of what is brutal, dark, and feral,
as a way of telling the full story of childhood.

To give a fierce new voice to our nightmares
and fears while returning to the irresistible
depths of the old stories: that mix of the
marvelous, magic, and turmoil.

To reimagine an age-old tapestry in my paintings,
inspired by the folk imagery of southern Italy
and Eastern Europe, along with the folk and
naïve arts of Europe's northern countries.

Rainer Maria Rilke wrote: "Beauty is nothing but
the beginning of terror."

This "terror" is something we can experience
at any age, with fascination and, I hope,
some delight.

—B.A.

FACE

inter.
A queen.
A queen who is not me,
and snowflakes falling
like downy feathers.

This queen is sewing in front of an open window.
The sight of the snowflakes dazzles her.
She pricks her finger, and three drops of blood
fall, embroidering a face on the snow.
The queen thinks: "If only the heavens would
give me a daughter, her complexion and lips
would look just like this."

It isn't long before she brings a baby girl
into the world, with skin as white as snow
and lips as red as blood. The child is graced
with a tremendous head of hair: a mane of
ebony, as sparkling as a starry night.

Hair of silk, marble, velvet.
Hair as thick as animal fur.
Goddess hair. Forest hair.

This girl is tearing out my heart.
She is the child I will never have.
She is the youth I have lost.
I am going mad. I have been dreaming of love
since I was a child. Of the love I never knew.
I hate all that is better than me.
I drape myself with diamonds, and anger.
I detest this child with all my heart.
Of thousands of possible names, they call
this princess Snow White.

But her mother the queen will soon die.
And the king will remarry.
Me. He will marry me.

It's my time to shine. Me, at last.
Me, the beloved, the beautiful,
the powerful.
Me, me, me.

But now the king has died, too.

I find myself alone with Snow White,
whom I banish from my quarters.
I never want to lay eyes on her again;
crossing paths with her is excruciating.

A magic mirror tells me everything.
Who is the most beautiful. Who.
One day, this mirror will be the death of me.

On that cursed day, the mirror will answer:
"You are very beautiful, Madame Queen, but
Snow White's beauty now surpasses your own."

O Moon, sky, ice, heavens. That day has come.
Standing on tiptoe, I see my certain death,
and let out the most terrible of cries.

My face takes on the color of a dried-up soul.
To die or to kill.
It will be me or her.
The blackbirds sing.
My heart is a ball of dirt.
I grow spikes. I'm covered in thorns.
I am a snarled vine that scratches.

I must send for my huntsman. I need
the cruelest one. The one who won't spare
the life of this child. I order him to take
Snow White into the forest and to bring
me back her liver and lungs. The huntsman
obeys and leads the girl into the woods.

s serene as spring, Snow White doesn't suspect a thing. The huntsman brings her to the darkest, most remote corner of the forest.

It's not until he draws his knife to pierce her pure heart that she finally understands his intent and bursts into tears.

She begs: "Good huntsman, don't kill me! I will run away into the woods and never return, I swear." She has nothing to sway him but her beauty, her terrible beauty, and the power of her wide, fearful eyes.

The huntsman takes pity on her: "Be off with you, poor child! The wild beasts will devour you, and you'll be dead soon enough."

With that cruel task lifted from his heart,
he knows what he must do. He attacks a
young boar, slaughters it, rips out its liver
and lungs, and brings them back to the palace
as proof of his loyalty.

Unaware of this trickery,
I eat them, chew them, swallow them.
I feel alive, renewed.

But the mirror soon tells me that Snow White
is not dead. She is alive, in the woods of
the seven mountains. She is fighting her way
through leaves and branches, running and
stumbling over brambles and jagged stones.
The wild beasts brush past her, but they leave
her alone, unharmed.

Snow White runs and runs, into the evening, until she can run no more. It is then that she notices an unusual house, hidden amidst the trees, and goes inside to rest.

Everything is grand and elegant. There is a table surrounded by seven chairs, and against the wall, there are seven little beds. Snow White eats what she can find. Then, exhausted, she falls into a deep sleep.

At twilight, the dwarves who live in the house return from work. By day, they pick and dig, mining the mountains for ore. As they come in, they light their candles and discover Snow White collapsed on a bed.

They approach her, astonished. As they get closer, they see her delicate hands and utter cries of wonder when they see her face.

"My god, this girl is beautiful!"

They feel such joy, they don't want to wake her. They watch her sleep until morning.

When Snow White does wake up, she is frightened by the crowd surrounding her. But the kind dwarves put her at ease, and ask her to tell them her story. Snow White tells them about the queen, the huntsman, everything. The dwarves invite Snow White to stay with them, and she accepts, with all her heart.

My heart fills with unspeakable pain.

I see Snow White is staying with the dwarves, keeping house for them. That means she spends her days alone. The good men warn her to watch out for me as they depart for the mountain. They tell her never to allow anyone inside the house, ever.

Meanwhile, I pace back and forth in my empty palace, full of dread. I ponder new ways to take the life of this creature.

I settle on one.

Disguised as an old peddler, I cross the seven mountains, find the house, and knock on the door, calling: "Beautiful goods for sale! Ribbons and lace in every color!"

Curious, Snow White unlocks the door, buys a bodice ribbon from me, and asks me to lace her up properly. That's when I tighten her bodice so violently that her chest almost cracks.

"There you are, my dear!" I shout. "All done... and dead!" I flee, wild with joy, leaving her body behind.

When the dwarves return, they find Snow White lifeless on the floor, and fear the worst. Lifting her up, they discover the lacing and quickly cut her free. Snow White takes a deep breath, and is revived.

The dwarves know this is my doing and admonish Snow White once more: "Do not let anyone enter here ever again, or you will surely die!"

ack at the palace, I hurry to ask the mirror if Snow White is finally gone. When I hear the truth, I am seized by terror.

"This time I will find the way to destroy you!" My vow rings out, loud and clear. I slip into a secret room and prepare a poisoned apple so deadly the tiniest morsel would kill her.

Dressed as an old peasant, I make my way back to the seven mountains. I knock on the door.
"I mustn't let anyone in. The dwarves said so," Snow White says firmly.
"That's fine with me, I just need to get rid of these apples."
"I am not allowed to accept anything, either," says Snow White.
"If you're afraid, my dear, I will share this apple with you: We'll each eat half."

She agrees, and we both take a bite, but since I cleverly poisoned only her portion, Snow White is the one who falls down dead.

With my fiercest glare, I hiss: "Now you are truly white...in death! The dwarves can't help you now!"

By the time I get home, I'm drunk with joy.
I question the mirror, and it finally responds:
"Madame Queen, from this day forward, you are
the most beautiful in the land."
O bells of the realm, ring out forever!
At long last, my jealous, wounded heart soars
to the skies.

That evening, the dwarves return to find Snow
White on the floor, unmoving. They lift her up
and try reviving her with rose water, but the
verdict is final: Death has taken her.

They circle around her and cry for three days.
As they solemnly prepare for her burial, they
notice that her complexion is as radiant as
if she were alive. "We cannot bury her in the
ground!" they exclaim together. So they build
a glass casket that allows them to admire her,
and her hair, from every side. And there they
place Snow White, with her name and title of
princess engraved in gold letters.

Ravaged by sorrow, the dwarves carry the casket
up the mountain, where they can guard it day
and night. The woods are frozen over.
The wild beasts come to mourn Snow White.

now White remains pristine in her casket for a very long time. Then one day a prince who is traveling through the forest spots this strange scene from afar. Upon his approach, he discovers Snow White in her frozen splendor.

He pleads with the dwarves: "Let me have this casket, for here lies the one I love!" The dwarves tell him they could never, ever give her up.

"I beg of you," implores the prince, "now that I've seen her face, I cannot live without her. I will honor and cherish her above all that is dear to me."

Deeply moved, the dwarves agree to give him Snow White.

The prince orders his servants to transport the casket. During the journey, one of them stumbles, jolting the body and dislodging the poisoned morsel from Snow White's mouth.

At that very instant, Snow White opens her eyes. She pushes open the casket and sits up, bewildered.

"You live! Death has spared you!" exclaims the incredulous prince.

Then he tells Snow White all about himself, and finishes by asking for her hand in marriage.

Stunned by life, and the dazzling sun, Snow White accepts without hesitation.

Their wedding is to be celebrated
with great ceremony. Even I am
invited to attend the festivities.

I decide to go. I must know everything.
I must face my jealousy once again.

As soon as I enter, Snow White's beauty
stops me cold.

They have been waiting for me.
Waiting with iron shoes,
heated up on blazing coals.

The shoes are for me.

With large tongs,
they pull them from the fire
and thrust them towards me.

I am forced to put them on.
I am forced to stand up and dance.

Feeling boundless pain,
in front of a merciless crowd.

Dancing with abandon,
spinning, swooning.

Extinguishing my fire,
facing the world as I am.

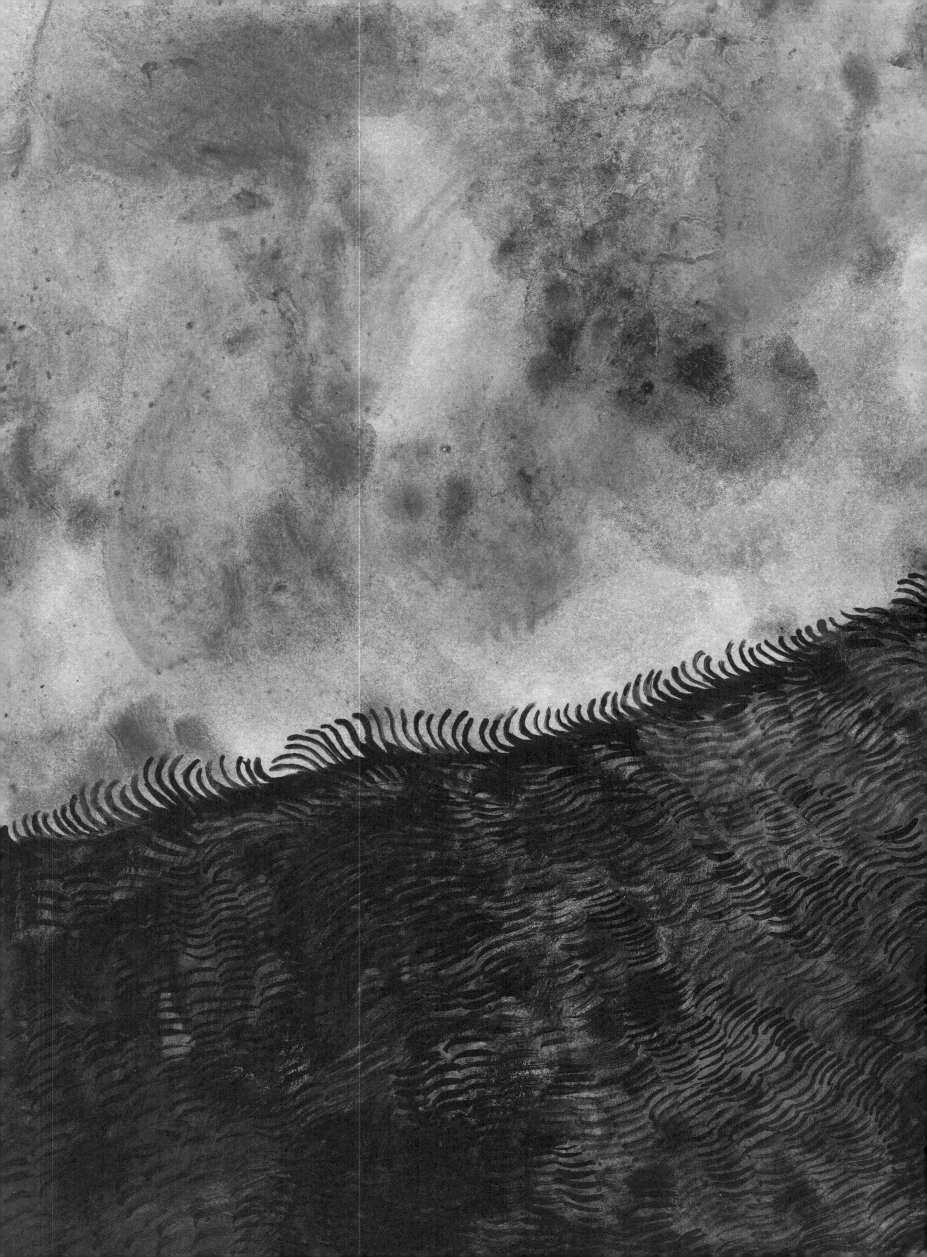

Becoming everything, again.

Earth.
Wind.
Cloud.
Stone.

Becoming nothing.